GOD OF WAR

B IS FOR BOY

WRITTEN BY ANDREA ROBINSON

ORIGINAL ILLUSTRATIONS BY ROMINA TEMPEST

INSIGHT
EDITIONS

SAN RAFAEL • LOS ANGELES • LONDON

AND SO, WE ARE ALONE NOW, JUST US TWO.
NO, I AM NOT AFRAID OF SPENDING TIME WITH MY SON. ARE YOU?

WE WILL USE THIS TIME FOR LESSONS.
LIKE **A** IS FOR **AXE,** STEADFAST AND TRUE.
AND **B** IS FOR **BOW,** WHICH YOUR MOTHER MADE FOR YOU.

C IS FOR **COME, BOY.** CONTROL YOUR ANGER, CLOSE YOUR HEART.
AND DO NOT TOUCH THAT FALLEN TROLL;
WE KNOW NOT WHERE IT HAS BEEN, FOR A START.

D IS FOR **DARK**, LIKE THE JOURNEY AHEAD . . .
WAIT! DO NOT JUST RUN OFF. YOU WILL END UP IN TROUBLE—OR DEAD.

WHOA!

E IS FOR **ENERGY**, YOURS IS MUCH GREATER THAN MINE.
WE WILL PLAY THE QUIET GAME, UNTIL WE REACH THE NEXT SHRINE.

F IS FOR **FREE WITH OUR BUSINESS**, WHICH YOU CERTAINLY ARE.
DO NOT TELL THIS WOMAN IN A TURTLE I HATE PEOPLE—THAT IS GOING TOO FAR.

H IS FOR **HER,** THE MEMORY BETWEEN US.
DO NOT MISTAKE MY SILENCE FOR LACK OF GRIEF—
IT IS NOT SOMETHING I WISH TO DISCUSS.

I IS FOR **IT WILL SERVE YOU TO STOP TALKING.**
NO, YOU CANNOT CARRY THE ASHES, BOY. KEEP WALKING.

FOR **J** IS FOR **JOURNEY,** BY NOW OURS HAS SURELY LASTED YEARS
. . . YOU SAY IT IS NOT EVEN HALF OVER? SOMEHOW, THAT IS NOT HOW IT FEELS.

K IS FOR KNIFE. DO NOT LOSE IT AGAIN.
THIS IS ALL YOU GET—THEY DO NOT GROW ON MOUNTAINS.

M IS FOR **MIMIR**, SMARTEST MAN BROUGHT LOW.
THIS SATYR IS FULL OF UNWANTED ADVICE AS WELL—WHAT DOES HE KNOW?

O IS FOR **ODIN,** ANOTHER PETTY GOD AND HIS MEDDLING PROGENY.
I BLAME A CYCLE OF BAD PARENTING WHEN IT COMES TO MAGNI AND MODI.

P IS FOR **PROTECT YOU**—FROM ENEMIES, FROM MY PAST.
BECAUSE THE THINGS I LEFT OUT ARE TOO DARK, TOO VAST.

Q IS FOR **QUIET, BOY.** THIS HAS SPIRALED QUICK.
YES, YOU ARE A GOD, BUT THAT IS NO EXCUSE TO BE A DICK.

WE'RE SICK OF HEARING ABOUT LITTLE PEOPLE'S PROBLEMS.

R IS FOR **RESPONSIBILITY,** OVER WEAPONS AND MIND.
YOU ARE POWERFUL, BUT WE MUST BE BETTER THAN ALL HUMANKIND.

S IS FOR **START OVER,** WHICH I WOULD LIKE TO DO.
THERE MUST BE GOOD GODS TO POINT OUT. I COUNT . . . MAYBE TWO.

LIKE **T** IS FOR **TÝR,** GOD OF WAR WHO FOUGHT FOR PEACE.
U IS FOR **UNDERSTAND?** THIS BEHAVIOR MUST CEASE.

THAT SYMBOL. IT'S A BUNCH OF RUNES TOGETHER. PEACE. UNITY. HOPE.

FOR IF V IS FOR VENGEANCE, NOTHING IS DOWN THAT PATH BUT DOOM.
(WHEN ALL THIS IS OVER, I AM GOING TO LIE DOWN IN A DARK ROOM.)
I GUESS WE'RE THE BAD GUYS NOW.

W is for **WHAT WOULD YOUR MOTHER SAY?** I would like to know.
WHAT DID SHE TEACH YOU? HOW DID SHE HELP YOU GROW?

X IS FOR **THAT BLANK SPACE SHE LEFT,** WITH NO ONE LEFT TO FILL, AFTER WE TRUDGE TO THE TOP OF THIS GIANTS' HILL.

EXCEPT FOR **Y** IS FOR **YOU,** WHO MAKES ME BETTER—
AND HAS ON THIS JOURNEY WITH EVERY LETTER.

SO, YOUR DAD WAS **Z** FOR **ZEUS?** THAT'S CONVENIENT.

INSIGHT EDITIONS

PO BOX 3088
SAN RAFAEL, CA 94912
WWW.INSIGHTEDITIONS.COM

FIND US ON FACEBOOK: WWW.FACEBOOK.COM/INSIGHTEDITIONS
FOLLOW US ON TWITTER: @INSIGHTEDITIONS

ISBN: 978-1-68383-889-0

PUBLISHER: RAOUL GOFF
PRESIDENT: KATE JEROME
ASSOCIATE PUBLISHER: VANESSA LOPEZ
CREATIVE DIRECTOR: CHRISSY KWASNIK
VP OF MANUFACTURING: ALIX NICHOLAEFF
DESIGNER: BROOKE MCCULLUM
EDITOR: AMANDA NG
EDITORIAL ASSISTANT: MAYA ALPERT
MANAGING EDITOR: LAUREN LEPERA
PRODUCTION EDITOR: JENNIFER BENTHAM
PRODUCTION MANAGER: EDEN ORLESKY

ROOTS of PEACE   REPLANTED PAPER

INSIGHT EDITIONS, IN ASSOCIATION WITH ROOTS OF PEACE, WILL PLANT TWO TREES FOR EACH TREE USED IN THE MANUFACTURING OF THIS BOOK. ROOTS OF PEACE IS AN INTERNATIONALLY RENOWNED HUMANITARIAN ORGANIZATION DEDICATED TO ERADICATING LAND MINES WORLDWIDE AND CONVERTING WAR-TORN LANDS INTO PRODUCTIVE FARMS AND WILDLIFE HABITATS. ROOTS OF PEACE WILL PLANT TWO MILLION FRUIT AND NUT TREES IN AFGHANISTAN AND PROVIDE FARMERS THERE WITH THE SKILLS AND SUPPORT NECESSARY FOR SUSTAINABLE LAND USE.

MANUFACTURED IN CHINA BY INSIGHT EDITIONS

10 9 8 7 6 5 4 3 2 1